For Rob, with love – S.A.H.

To Mum and Dad,
with love – J.C.

Dorling Kindersley Publishing, Inc.
95 Madison Avenue,
New York, New York 10016

Text copyright © 2000 by Sandra Ann Horn
Illustrations copyright © 2000 by Jason Cockcroft

A catalog record is available from the Library of Congress.

ISBN 0-7894-6326-1

Color reproduction by Dot Gradations, UK
Printed and bound by L. Rex in China

First American Edition, 2000

2 4 6 8 10 9 7 5 3 1

First published in Great Britain in 2000 by
Dorling Kindersley Limited.

see our complete
catalog at
www.dk.com

The Dandelion Wish

Sandra Ann Horn ✳ Illustrated by Jason Cockcroft

Dorling Kindersley Publishing, Inc.

The summer drifted on as if it would never end. The days were warm and long in the dandelion field where Sam and Jo played.

"What shall we do today?" asked Jo. "We've played every game we know a hundred times or more."

Just then a breeze blew over the field and tossed the
dandelion seeds up into the air.
Sam said, "My granny says you can make a wish
if you blow all the seeds in one breath."
"But do wishes come true?" asked Jo.
"Maybe if you wish hard enough they do," said Sam.

They each picked a silver dandelion head,
took a deep breath, and blew —
up and away every seed flew!
Sam and Jo whispered a secret wish
as they watched the seeds fly high.
Nobody heard it but the breeze and the feathery seeds
as they soared through the sky.

The seeds flew up and over the hedge
and away down Rooster Lane,
past all the houses, once around the duck pond,
and disappeared from view.
"Where are they going?" asked Jo.
"To bring us our wish," said Sam. "You'll see."

They waited. And waited. They counted to ten. They counted to ten again.

"I don't think it worked," said Jo.

Then, "Listen!" said Sam. "Can you hear?"

Jo heard music on the breeze,
coming closer and closer every minute,
wagon wheels turning, many feet marching,
ding ding ding and *om-tiddley-pom!*

Sam and Jo ran to the gate to look.
There in the lane were banners waving,
balloons bobbing,
and a baton gleaming gold in the sun.
"What is it?" asked Sam.
"I think it's our wish," said Jo.

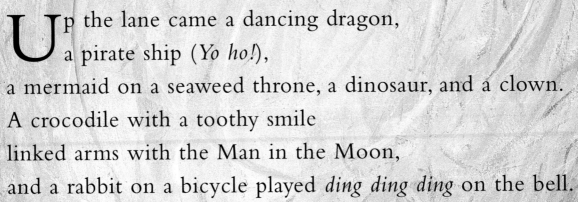

Up the lane came a dancing dragon,
a pirate ship (*Yo ho!*),
a mermaid on a seaweed throne, a dinosaur, and a clown.
A crocodile with a toothy smile
linked arms with the Man in the Moon,
and a rabbit on a bicycle played *ding ding ding* on the bell.

"Please open the gate!" called the rabbit,
"and let the carnival come in!"

Sam and Jo hurried to pull back the gate,
and in marched the grand parade.
Then out of the wagons came, wonder on wonder —
a ring toss, a cake walk, a man on tree-high stilts,
a puppet show in a striped tent, and more and more and more.
"It's the dandelion carnival!" said Jo.
"Our wish has come true!" said Sam.

"Come and join the fun!" called the rabbit.
The dinosaur gave them each a giant red balloon.
The pirates hollered, "Come aboard, mateys!
There's popcorn and lemonade (*Yo ho!*)."
Then they ran in a three-legged race
with the clown and the Man in the Moon.
The Moon fell down and tripped up the clown,
and Sam and Jo laughed till they fell down, too!

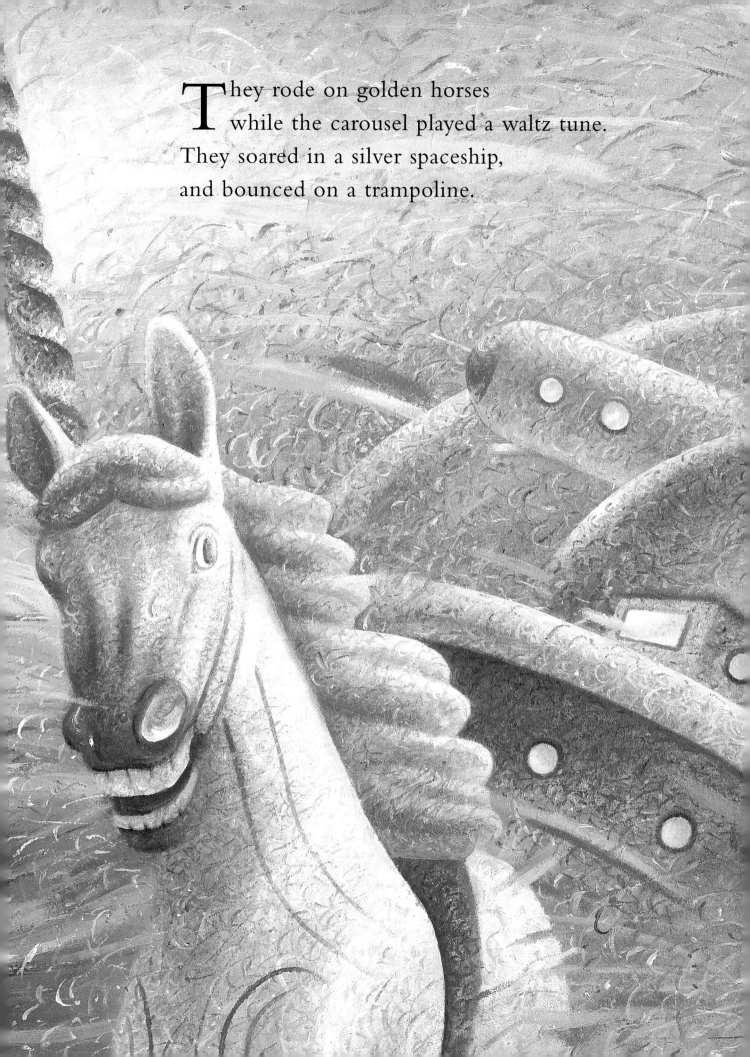

They rode on golden horses
   while the carousel played a waltz tune.
They soared in a silver spaceship,
and bounced on a trampoline.

All the bright day the fun went on,
till the shadows grew deep and long.
Then as dusk crept over the field,
and the setting sun flamed red,
a bonfire was lit, the old songs were sung,
and fireworks spangled the sky.

Jo and Sam waved to the pirate ship
as they were carried home to bed,
sleepily over the dandelion field,
under the summer moon.
Only the owls saw the bonfire die
and the crocodile creep down the lane.
Only the night heard a home-going rabbit
whistling a rock-a-bye tune.

Early the next morning the children
came running into the dandelion field –
but the carnival had gone!
The dragon had vanished, the dinosaur, too,
and so had the clown and the Man in the Moon.
"I wish the carnival would come back," said Jo.

Just then a breeze danced over the field. . . .

. . .And it blew ALL the seeds up into the air!
The silvery seeds floated up on the breeze,
cloud upon cloud of them,
jiggling and swirling like summery snow.
"There must be a million at least!" cried Sam.
"Hurry! Let's make a wish!" said Jo.
So they danced through the seed–cloud
and whispered their wishes.

A dandelion wish is a wish to come true,
and million-seed wishes always do!